BOOT HILL PAYOFF
(THE LAST RIDE)

BY

ROBERT E. HOWARD

British Library Cataloguing-in-Publication Data
A catalogue record for this book is available from the
British Library

Contents

Robert E. Howard

Robert Ervin Howard was born in Peaster, Texas in 1906. During his youth, his family moved between a variety of Texan boomtowns, and Howard – a bookish and somewhat introverted child – was steeped in the violent myths and legends of the Old South. Although he loved reading and learning, Howard developed a distinctly Texan, hardboiled outlook on the world. He became a passionate fan of boxing, taking it up at an amateur level, and from the age of nine began to write adventure tales of semi-historical bloodshed. In 1919, when Howard was thirteen, his family moved to the Central Texas hamlet of Cross Plains, where he would stay for the rest of his life.

At fifteen Howard began to read the pulp magazines of the day, and to write more seriously. The December 1922 issue of his high school newspaper featured two of his stories, 'Golden Hope Christmas' and 'West is West'. In 1924 he sold his first piece – a short caveman tale titled 'Spear and Fang' – for $16 to the not-yet-famous *Weird Tales* magazine. He published with the magazine regularly over the next few years. 1929 was a breakout year for Howard, in that the 23-year-old writer began to sell to other magazines, such as *Ghost Stories* and *Argosy*, both of whom had previously sent him hundreds of rejection slips. In 1930, he began a correspondence with weird fiction master H. P. Lovecraft which ran up to his death six years later, and is regarded as one of the great correspondence cycles in all of fantasy literature.

It was partly due to Lovecraft's encouragement that Howard created his most famous character, Conan the Cimmerian. Conan – a barbarian-turned-King during the Hyborian Age, a mythical period of some 12,000 years ago – featured in seventeen *Weird Tales* stories between 1933 and 1936, and is now regarded as having spawned the 'sword and sorcery' genre, making Howard's influence on fantasy literature comparable to that of J. R. R. Tolkien's. The Conan stories have since been adapted many times, most famously in the series of films starring Arnold Schwarzenegger.

Howard was enjoying an all-time high in sales by the beginning of 1936, but he was also deeply upset by the ill health of his mother, who had fallen into a coma. On the morning of June 11, 1936, he asked an attending nurse whether she would ever recover, and the nurse replied negatively. Howard walked to his car, parked outside the family home in Cross Plains, and shot himself. He died eight hours later, aged just thirty.

CHAPTER I:
THE LARAMIES RIDE

Five men were riding down the winding road that led to San Leon, and one was singing, in a toneless monotone:

"Early in the mornin' in the month of May,
Brady came down on the mornin' train.
Brady came down on the Shinin' Star.
And he shot Mr. Duncan in behind the bar!

"Shut up! Shut up!" It was the youngest of the riders who ripped out like that. A lanky, tow-headed kid, with a touch of pallor under his tan, and a rebellious smolder in his hot eyes.

The biggest man of the five grinned.

"Bucky's nervous," he jeered genially. "You don't want to be no derned bandit, do you, Bucky?"

The youngest glowered at him.

"That welt on yore jaw ought to answer that, Jim," he growled.

"You fit like a catamount," agreed Big Jim placidly. "I thought we'd never git you on yore cayuse and started for San Leon, without knockin' you in the head. 'Bout the only way you show yo're a Laramie, Bucky, is in the handlin' of yore fists."

"T'ain't no honor to be a Laramie," flared Bucky. "You and Luke and Tom and Hank has dragged the name through slime. For the last three years you been worse'n a pack of starvin' lobos--stealin' cattle and horses; robbin' folks--why, the country's near ruint. And now yo're headin' to San Leon to put on the final touch--robbin' the Cattlemen's Bank, when you know dern well the help the ranchmen got from that bank's been all that kept 'em on their feet. Old man Brown's stretched hisself nigh to the bustin' p'int to help folks."

He gulped and fought back tears that betrayed his extreme youth. His brothers grinned tolerantly. "It's the last time," he informed them bitterly. "You won't git me into no raid again!"

"It's the last time for all of us," said Big Jim, biting off a cud of tobacco. "We're through after this job. We'll live like honest men in Mexico."

"Serve you right if a posse caught us and hanged us all," said Bucky viciously.

"Not a chance." Big Jim's placidity was unruffled. "Nobody but us knows the trail that follows the secret waterholes acrost the desert. No posse'd dare to foller us. Once out of town and headed south for the border, the devil hisself couldn't catch us."

"I wonder if anybody'll ever stumble onto our secret hide-out up in the Los Diablos Mountains," mused Hank.

"I doubt it. Too well hid. Like the desert trail, nobody but us knows them mountain trails. It shore served us well. Think of all the steers and horses we've hid there, and drove through the mountains to Mexico! And the times we've laid up there laughin' in our sleeves as the posse chased around a circle."

Bucky muttered something under his breath; he retained no fond memories of that hidden lair high up in the barren Diablos. Three years before, he had reluctantly followed his brothers into it from the little ranch in the foothills where Old Man Laramie and his wife had worn away their lives in futile work. The old life, when their parents lived and had held their wild sons in check, had been drab and hard, but had lacked the bitterness he had known when cooking and tending house for his brothers in that hidden den from which they had ravaged the countryside. Four good men gone bad--mighty bad.

San Leon lay as if slumbering in the desert heat as the five brothers rode up to the doors of the Cattlemen's Bank. None noted their coming; the Red Lode saloon, favorite rendezvous for the masculine element of San Leon, stood at the other end of the town, and out of sight around a slight bend in the street.

No words were passed; each man knew his part beforehand. The three elder Laramies slid lithely out of their saddles, throwing their reins to Bucky and Luke, the second youngest. They strode into the bank with a soft jingle of spurs and creak of leather, closing the door behind them.

Luke's face was impassive as an image's, as he dragged leisurely on a cigarette, though his eyes gleamed between slitted lids. But Bucky sweated and shivered, twisting nervously in his saddle. By some twist of destiny, one son had inherited all the honesty that was his parents' to transmit. He had kept his hands clean. Now, in spite of himself, he was scarred with their brand.

He started convulsively as a gun crashed inside the bank; like an echo came another reverberation.

Luke's Colt was in his hand, and he snatched one foot clear of the stirrup, then feet pounded toward the street and the door burst open to emit the three outlaws. They carried bulging canvas sacks, and Hank's sleeve was crimson.

"Ride like hell!" grunted Big Jim, forking his roan. "Old Brown throwed down on Hank. Old fool! I had to salivate him permanent."

And like hell it was they rode, straight down the street toward the desert, yelling and firing as they went. They thundered past houses from which startled individuals peered bewilderedly, past stores where leathery faced storekeepers were dragging forth blue-barreled scatter-guns. They swept through the futile rain of lead that poured from the excited and befuddled crowd in front of the Red Lode, and whirled on toward the desert that stretched south of San Leon.

But not quite to the desert. For as they rounded the last bend in the twisting street and came abreast of the last house in the village, they were confronted by the gray-bearded figure of old "Pop" Anders, sheriff of San Leon County. The old man's gnarled right hand rested on the ancient single-action Colt on his thigh, his left was lifted in a seemingly futile command to halt.

Big Jim cursed and sawed back on the reins, and the big roan slid to a halt.

"Git outa the way, Pop!" roared Big Jim. "We don't want to hurt you."

The old warrior's eyes blazed with righteous wrath.

"Robbed the bank this time, eh?" he said in cold fury, his eyes on the canvas sacks. "Likely spilt blood, too. Good thing Frank Laramie died before he could know what skunks his boys turned out to be. You ain't content to steal our stock till we're nigh bankrupt; you got to rob our bank and take what little money we got left for a new start. Why, you damned human sidewinders!" the old man shrieked, his control snapping suddenly. "Ain't there nothin' that's too low-down for you to do?"

Behind them sounded the pound of running feet and a scattering banging of guns. The crowd from the Red Lode was closing in.

"You've wasted our time long enough, old man!" roared Luke, jabbing in the spurs and sending his horse rearing and plunging toward the indomitable figure. "Git outa the way, or--"

The old single-action jumped free in the gnarled hand. Two shots roared together, and Luke's sombrero went skyrocketing from his head. But the old sheriff fell face forward in the dust with a bullet through his heart, and the Laramie gang swept on into the desert, feeding their dust to their hurriedly mounted and disheartened pursuers.

Only young Buck Laramie looked back, to see the door of the last house fly open, and a pig-tailed girl run out to the still figure in the street. It was the sheriff's daughter, Judy. She and Buck had gone to the same school in the old days before the Laramies hit the wolf-trail. Buck had always been her champion. Now she went down on her knees in the dust beside her father's body, seeking frantically for a spark of life where there was none.

A red film blazed before Buck Laramie's eyes as he turned his livid face toward his brothers.

"Hell," Luke was fretting, "I didn't aim to salivate him permanent. The old lobo woulda hung everyone of us if he could of--but just the same I didn't aim to kill him."

8

Something snapped in Bucky's brain.

"You didn't aim to kill him!" he shrieked. "No, but you did! Yo're all a pack of low-down sidewinders just like he said! They ain't nothin' too dirty for you!" He brandished his clenched fists in the extremity of his passion. "You filthy scum!" he sobbed. "When I'm growed up I'm comin' back here and make up for ever' dollar you've stole, ever' life you've took. I'll do it if they hang me for tryin', s'help me!"

His brothers did not reply. They did not look at him. Big Jim hummed flatly and absently:

"Some say he shot him with a thirty-eight,

Some say he shot him with a forty-one;

But I say he shot him with a forty-four.

For I saw him as he lay on the barroom floor."

Bucky subsided, slumped in his saddle and rode dismally on. San Leon and the old life lay behind them all. Somewhere south of the hazy horizon the desert stretched into Mexico where lay their future destiny. And his destiny was inextricably interwoven with that of his brothers. He was an outlaw, too, now, and he must stay with the clan to the end of their last ride.

Some guiding angel must have caused Buck Laramie to lean forward to pat the head of his tired sorrel, for at that instant a bullet ripped through his hat-brim, instead of his head.

It came as a startling surprise, but his reaction was instant. He leaped from his horse and dove for the protection of a sand bank, a second bullet spurting dust at his heels. Then he was under cover, peering warily out, Colt in hand.

The tip of a white sombrero showed above a rim of sand, two hundred yards in front of him. Laramie blazed away at it, though knowing as he pulled the trigger that the range was too long and the target too small for six-gun accuracy. Nevertheless, the hat-top vanished.

"Takin' no chances," muttered Laramie. "Now who in hell is he? Here I am a good hour's ride from San Leon, and folks pottin' at me already. Looks bad for what I'm aimin' to do. Reckon it's somebody that knows me, after all these years?"

He could not believe it possible that anyone would recognize the lanky, half-grown boy of six years ago in the bronzed, range-hardened man who was returning to San Leon to keep the vow he had made as his clan rode southward with two dead men and a looted bank behind them.

The sun was burning hot, and the sand felt like an oven beneath Laramie. His canteen was slung to his saddle, and his horse was out of his reach, drooping under a scrubby mesquite. The other fellow would eventually work around to a point where his rifle would out-range Laramie's six-gun- -or he might shoot the horse and leave Buck afoot in the desert.

10

The instant his attacker's next shot sang past his refuge, he was up and away in a stooping, weaving run to the next sand hill, to the right and slightly forward of his original position. He wanted to get in close quarters with his unknown enemy.

He wriggled from cover to cover, and sprinted in short dashes over narrow strips of open ground, taking advantage of every rock, cactus-bed and sand-bank, with lead hissing and spitting at him all the way. The hidden gunman had guessed his purpose, and obviously had no desire for a close-range fight. He was slinging lead every time Laramie showed an inch of flesh, cloth or leather, and Buck counted the shots. He was within striking distance of the sand rim when he believed the fellow's rifle was empty.

Springing recklessly to his feet he charged straight at his hidden enemy, his six-gun blazing. He had miscalculated about the rifle, for a bullet tore through the slack of his shirt. But then the Winchester was silent, and Laramie was raking the rim with such a barrage of lead that the gunman evidently dared not lift himself high enough to line the sights of a six-gun.

But a pistol was something that must be reckoned with, and as he spent his last bullet, Laramie dove behind a rise of sand and began desperately to jam cartridges into his empty gun. He had failed to cross the sand rim in that rush, but another try would gain it--unless hot lead cut him down on the way. Drum of hoofs reached his ears suddenly and glaring over his shelter he saw a pinto pony beyond the sand rim heading in the direction of San Leon. Its rider wore a white sombrero.

"Damn!" Laramie slammed the cylinder in place and sent a slug winging after the rapidly receding horseman. But he did not repeat the shot. The fellow was already out of range.

"Reckon the work was gettin' too close for him," he ruminated as he trudged back to his horse. "Hell, maybe he didn't want me to get a good look at him. But why? Nobody in these parts would be shy about shootin' at a Laramie, if they knew him as such. But who'd know I was a Laramie?"

He swung up into the saddle, then absently slapped his saddle bags and the faint clinking that resulted soothed him. Those bags were loaded with fifty thousand dollars in gold eagles, and every penny was meant for the people of San Leon.

"It'll help pay the debt the Laramies owe for the money the boys stole," he confided to the uninterested sorrel. "How I'm goin' to pay back for the men they killed is more'n I can figure out. But I'll try."

The money represented all he had accumulated from the sale of the Laramie stock and holdings in Mexico--holdings bought with money stolen from San Leon. It was his by right of inheritance, for he was the last of the Laramies. Big Jim,

Tom, Hank, Luke, all had found trail's end in that lawless country south of the Border. As they had lived, so had they died, facing their killers, with smoking guns in their hands. They had tried to live straight in Mexico, but the wild blood was still there. Fate had dealt their hands, and Buck looked upon it all as a slate wiped clean, a record closed--with the exception of Luke's fate.

That memory vaguely troubled him now, as he rode toward San Leon to pay the debts his brothers contracted.

"Folks said Luke drew first," he muttered. "But it wasn't like him to pick a barroom fight. Funny the fellow that killed him cleared out so quick, if it was a fair fight."

He dismissed the old problem and reviewed the recent attack upon himself.

"If he knowed I was a Laramie, it might have been anybody. But how could he know? Joel Waters wouldn't talk."

No, Joel Waters wouldn't talk; and, Joel Waters, old time friend of Laramie's father, long ago, and owner of the Boxed W ranch, was the only man who knew Buck Laramie was returning to San Leon.

"San Leon at last, cayuse," he murmured as he topped the last desert sand hill that sloped down to the town. "Last time I seen it was under circumstances most--what the devil!"

13

He started and stiffened as a rattle of gunfire burst on his ears. Battle in San Leon? He urged his weary steed down the hill. Two minutes later history was repeating itself.

CHAPTER II:
OWL-HOOT GHOSTS

As Buck Laramie galloped into San Leon, a sight met his eyes which jerked him back to a day six years gone. For tearing down the street came six wild riders, yelling and shooting. In the lead rode one, who, with his huge frame and careless ease, might have been Big Jim Laramie come back to life again. Behind them the crowd at the Red Lode, roused to befuddled life, was shooting just as wildly and ineffectively as on that other day when hot lead raked San Leon. There was but one man to bar the bandits' path--one man who stood, legs braced wide, guns drawn, in the roadway before the last house in San Leon. So old Pop Anders had stood, that other day, and there was something about this man to remind Laramie of the old sheriff, though he was much younger. In a flash of recognition Laramie knew him--Bob Anders, son of Luke's victim. He, too, wore a silver star.

This time Laramie did not stand helplessly by to see a sheriff slaughtered. With the swiftness born of six hard years below the border, he made his decision and acted. Gravel spurted as the sorrel threw back his head against the sawing bit and came to a sliding stop, and all in one motion Laramie was out of the saddle and on his feet beside the sheriff--half crouching and his six-gun cocked and pointed. This time two would meet the charge, not one.

Laramie saw that masks hid the faces of the riders as they swept down, and contempt stabbed through him. No Laramie ever wore a mask. His Colt vibrated as he thumbed the hammer. Beside him the young sheriff's guns were spitting smoke and lead.

The clumped group split apart at that blast. One man, who wore a Mexican sash instead of a belt, slumped in his saddle clawing for the horn. Another with his right arm flopping broken at his side was fighting his pain-maddened beast which had stopped a slug intended for its rider.

The big man who had led the charge grabbed the fellow with the sash as he started to slide limply from his saddle, and dragged him across his own bow. He bolted across the roadside and plunged into a dry wash. The others followed him. The man with the broken arm abandoned his own crazed mount and grabbed the reins of the riderless horse. Beasts and men, they slid over the rim and out of sight in a cloud of dust.

Anders yelled and started across the road on the run, but Laramie jerked him back.

"They're covered," he grunted, sending his sorrel galloping to a safe place with a slap on the rump. "We got to get out of sight, pronto!"

The sheriff's good judgment overcame his excitement then, and he wheeled and darted for the house, yelping: "Follow me, stranger!"

Bullets whined after them from the gulch as the outlaws began their stand. The door opened inward before Anders' outstretched hand touched it, and he plunged through without checking his stride. Lead smacked the jambs and splinters flew as Laramie ducked after Anders. He collided with something soft and yielding that gasped and tumbled to the floor under the impact. Glaring wildly down Laramie found himself face to face with a vision of feminine loveliness that took his breath away, even in that instant. With a horrified gasp he plunged to his feet and lifted the girl after him. His all-embracing gaze took her in from tousled blond hair to whipcord breeches and high-heeled riding boots. She seemed too bewildered to speak.

"Sorry, miss," he stuttered. "I hope y'ain't hurt. I was--I was--" The smash of a window pane and the whine of a bullet cut short his floundering apologies. He snatched the girl out of line of the window and in an instant was crouching beside it himself, throwing lead across the road toward the smoke wisps.

Anders had barred the door and grabbed a Winchester from a rack on the wall.

"Duck into a back room, Judy," he ordered, kneeling at the window on the other side of the door. "Partner, I don't know you--" he punctuated his remarks with rapid shots, "--but I'm plenty grateful."

"Hilton's the name," mumbled Laramie, squinting along, his six-gun barrel. "Friends call me Buck--damn!"

His bullet had harmlessly knocked dust on the gulch rim, and his pistol was empty. As he groped for cartridges he felt a Winchester pushed into his hand, and, startled, turned his head to stare full into the disturbingly beautiful face of Judy Anders. She had not obeyed her brother's order, but had taken a loaded rifle from the rack and brought it to Laramie, crossing the room on hands and knees to keep below the line of fire. Laramie almost forgot the men across the road as he stared into her deep clear eyes, now glowing with excitement. In dizzy fascination he admired the peach-bloom of her cheeks, her red, parted lips.

"Th-thank you, miss!" he stammered. "I needed that smoke-wagon right smart. And excuse my language. I didn't know you was still in the room--"

He ducked convulsively as a bullet ripped across the sill, throwing splinters like a buzz-saw. Shoving the Winchester out of the window he set to work. But his mind was still addled. And he was remembering a pitifully still figure sprawled in the dust of that very road, and a pig-tailed child on her knees beside it. The child was no longer a child, but a beautiful woman; and he--he was still a Laramie, and the brother of the man who killed her father.

"Judy!" There was passion in Bob Anders' voice. "Will you get out of here? There! Somebody's callin' at the back door. Go let 'em in. And stay back there, will you?"

This time she obeyed, and a few seconds later half a dozen pairs of boots clomped into the room, as some men from the Red Lode who had slipped around through a back route to the besieged cabin, entered.

"They was after the bank, of course," announced one of them. "They didn't git nothin' though, dern 'em. Ely Harrison started slingin' lead the minute he seen them masks comin' in the door. He didn't hit nobody, and by good luck the lead they throwed at him didn't connect, but they pulled out in a hurry. Harrison shore s'prised me. I never thought much of him before now, but he showed he was ready to fight for his money, and our'n."

"Same outfit, of course," grunted the sheriff, peering warily through the jagged shards of the splintered window-pane.

"Sure. The damn' Laramies again. Big Jim leadin', as usual."

Buck Laramie jumped convulsively, doubting the evidence of his ears. He twisted his head to stare at the men.

"You think it's the Laramies out there?" Buck's brain felt a bit numb. These mental jolts were coming too fast for him.

"Sure," grunted Anders. "Couldn't be nobody else. They'was gone for six year--where, nobody knowed. But a few weeks back they showed up again and started their old deviltry, worse than ever."

"Killed his old man right out there in front of his house," grunted one of the men, selecting a rifle from the rack. The others were firing carefully through the windows, and the men in the gulch were replying in kind. The room was full of drifting smoke.

"But I've heard of 'em," Laramie protested. "They was all killed down in Old Mexico."

"Couldn't be," declared the sheriff, lining his sights. "These are the old gang all right. They've put up warnin's signed with the Laramie name. Even been heard singin' that old song they used to always sing about King Brady. Got a hide-out up in the Los Diablos, too, just like they did before. Same one, of course. I ain't managed to find it yet, but--" His voice was drowned in the roar of his .45-70.

"Well, I'll be a hammer-headed jackass," muttered Laramie under his breath. "Of all the--"

His profane meditations were broken into suddenly as one of the men bawled: "Shootin's slowed down over there! What you reckon it means?"

"Means they're aimin' to sneak out of that wash at the other end and high-tail it into the desert," snapped Anders. "I ought to have thought about that before, but things has been happenin' so fast. You hombres stay here and keep smokin' the wash so they can't bolt out on this side. I'm goin' to circle around and block 'em from the desert."

"I'm with you," growled Laramie. "I want to see what's behind them masks."

They ducked out the back way and began to cut a wide circle which should bring them to the outer edge of the wash. It was difficult going and frequently they had to crawl on their hands and knees to take advantage of every clump of cactus and greasewood.

"Gettin' purty close," muttered Laramie, lifting his head. "What I'm wonderin' is, why ain't they already bolted for the desert? Nothin' to stop 'em."

"I figger they wanted to get me if they could, before they lit out," answered Anders. "I believe I been snoopin' around in the Diablos too close to suit 'em. Look out! They've seen us!"

Both men ducked as a steady line of flame spurts rimmed the edge of the wash. They flattened down behind their scanty cover and bullets cut up puffs of sand within inches of them.

"This is a pickle!" gritted Anders, vainly trying to locate a human head to shoot at. "If we back up, we back into sight, and if we go forward we'll get perforated."

"And if we stay here the result's the same," returned Laramie. "Greasewood don't stop lead. We got to summon reinforcements." And lifting his voice in a stentorian yell that carried far, he whooped: "Come on, boys! Rush 'em from that side! They can't shoot two ways at once!"

They could not see the cabin from where they lay, but a burst of shouts and shots told them his yell had been heard. Guns began to bang up the wash and Laramie and Anders recklessly leaped to their feet and rushed down the slight slope that led to the edge of the gulch, shooting as they went.

They might have been riddled before they had gone a dozen steps, but the outlaws had recognized the truth of Laramie's statement. They couldn't shoot two ways at once, and they feared to be trapped in the gulch with attackers on each side. A few hurried shots buzzed about the ears of the charging men, and then outlaws burst into view at the end of the wash farthest from town, mounted and spurring hard, the big leader still carrying a limp figure across his saddle.

Cursing fervently, the sheriff ran after them, blazing away with both six-shooters, and Laramie followed him. The fleeing men were shooting backward as they rode, and the roar of six-guns and Winchesters was deafening. One of the men reeled in his saddle and caught at his shoulder, dyed suddenly red.

Laramie's longer legs carried him past the sheriff, but he did not run far. As the outlaws pulled out of range, toward the desert and the Diablos, he slowed to a walk and began reloading his gun.

"Let's round up the men, Bob," he called. "We'll follow 'em. I know the water-holes--"

He stopped short with a gasp. Ten yards behind him Bob Anders, a crimson stream dyeing the side of his head, was sinking to the desert floor.

Laramie started back on a run just as the men from the cabin burst into view. In their lead rode a man on a pinto-- and Buck Laramie knew that pinto.

"Git him!" howled the white-hatted rider. "He shot Bob Anders in the back! I seen him! He's a Laramie!"

Laramie stopped dead in his tracks. The accusation was like a bomb-shell exploding in his face. That was the man who had tried to drygulch him an hour or so before--same pinto, same white sombrero--but he was a total stranger to Laramie. How in the devil did he know of Buck's identity, and what was the reason for his enmity?

Laramie had no time to try to figure it out now. For the excited townsmen, too crazy with excitement to stop and think, seeing only their young sheriff stretched in his blood, and hearing the frantic accusation of one of their fellows, set up a roar and started blazing away at the man they believed was a murderer.

Out of the frying pan into the fire--the naked desert was behind him, and his horse was still standing behind the Anders' cabin--with that mob between him and that cabin.

But any attempt at explanation would be fatal. Nobody would listen. Laramie saw a break for him in the fact that only his accuser was mounted, and probably didn't know he had a horse behind the cabin, and would try to reach it. The others were too excited to think anything. They were simply slinging lead, so befuddled with the mob impulse they were not even aiming--which is all that saved Laramie in the few seconds in which he stood bewildered and uncertain.

He ducked for the dry wash, running almost at a right angle with his attackers. The only man capable of intercepting him was White-Hat, who was bearing down on him, shooting from the saddle with a Winchester.

Laramie wheeled, and as he wheeled a bullet ripped through his Stetson and stirred his hair in passing. White-Hat was determined to have his life, he thought, as his own six-gun spat flame. White-Hat flinched sidewise and dropped his rifle. Laramie took the last few yards in his stride and dived out of sight in the wash.

He saw White-Hat spurring out of range too energetically to be badly wounded, and he believed his bullet had merely knocked the gun out of the fellow's hands. The others had spread out and were coming down the slope at a run, burning powder as they came.

Laramie did not want to kill any of those men. They were law-abiding citizens acting under a misapprehension. So he emptied his gun over their heads and was gratified to see them precipitately take to cover. Then without pausing to reload, he ducked low and ran for the opposite end of the wash, which ran on an angle that would bring him near the cabin.

The men who had halted their charge broke cover and came on again, unaware of his flight, and hoping to get him while his gun was empty. They supposed he intended making a stand at their end of the wash.

By the time they had discovered their mistake and were pumping lead down the gully, Laramie was out at the other end and racing across the road toward the cabin. He ducked around the corner with lead nipping at his ears and vaulted into the saddle of the sorrel--and cursed his luck as Judy Anders ran out the rear door, her eyes wide with fright.

"What's happened?" she cried. "Where's Bob?"

"No time to pow-wow," panted Laramie. "Bob's been hurt. Don't know how bad. I got to ride, because--"

He was interrupted by shouts from the other side of the cabin.

"Look out, Judy!" one man yelled. "Stay under cover! He shot Bob in the back!"

Reacting to the shout without conscious thought, Judy sprang to seize his reins.

Laramie jerked the sorrel aside and evaded her grasp. "It's a lie!" he yelled with heat. "I ain't got time to explain. Hope Bob ain't hurt bad."

Then he was away, crouching low in his saddle with bullets pinging past him; it seemed he'd been hearing lead whistle all day; he was getting sick of that particular noise. He looked back once. Behind the cabin Judy Anders was bending over a limp form that the men had carried in from the desert. Now she was down on her knees in the dust beside that limp body, searching for a spark of life.

Laramie cursed sickly. History was indeed repeating itself that day in San Leon.

For a time Laramie rode eastward, skirting the desert, and glad of a breathing spell. The sorrel had profited by its rest behind the Anders' cabin, and was fairly fresh. Laramie had a good lead on the pursuers he knew would be hot on his trail as soon as they could get to their horses, but he headed east instead of north, the direction in which lay his real goal- -the Boxed W ranch. He did not expect to be able to throw them off his scent entirely, but he did hope to confuse them and gain a little time.

It was imperative that he see his one friend in San Leon County--Joel Waters. Maybe Joel Waters could unriddle some of the tangle. Who were the men masquerading as Laramies?

He had been forging eastward for perhaps an hour when, looking backward from a steep rise, he saw a column of riders approaching some two miles away through a cloud of dust that meant haste. That would be the posse following his trail--and that meant that the sheriff was dead or still senseless.

Laramie wheeled down the slope on the other side and headed north, hunting hard ground that would not betray a pony's hoof-print.

CHAPTER III:
TRIGGER DEBT

Dusk was fast settling when he rode into the yard of the Boxed W. He was glad of the darkness, for he had feared that some of Waters' punchers might have been in San Leon that day, and seen him. But he rode up to the porch without having encountered anyone, and saw the man he was hunting sitting there, pulling at a corn-cob pipe.

Waters rose and came forward with his hand outstretched as Laramie swung from the saddle.

"You've growed," said the old man. "I'd never knowed you if I hadn't been expectin' you. You don't favor yore brothers none. Look a lot like yore dad did at yore age, though. You've pushed yore cayuse hard," he added, with a piercing glance at the sweat-plastered flanks of the sorrel.

"Yeah." There was bitter humor in Laramie's reply. "I just got through shootin' me a sheriff."

Waters jerked the pipe from his mouth. He looked stunned.

"What?"

"All you got to do is ask the upright citizens of San Leon that's trailin' me like a lobo wolf," returned Laramie with a mirthless grin. And tersely and concisely he told the old rancher what had happened in San Leon and on the desert.

Waters listened in silence, puffing smoke slowly.

"It's bad," he muttered, when Laramie had finished. "Damned bad--well, about all I can do right now is to feed you. Put yore cayuse in the corral."

"Rather hide him near the house, if I could," said Laramie. "That posse is liable to hit my sign and trail me here any time. I want to be ready to ride."

"Blacksmith shop behind the house," grunted Waters. "Come on."

Laramie followed the old man to the shop, leading the sorrel. While he was removing the bridle and loosening the cinch, Waters brought hay and filled an old log-trough. When Laramie followed him back to the house, the younger man carried the saddle bags over his arm. Their gentle clink no longer soothed him; too many obstacles to distributing them were rising in his path.

"I just finished eatin' before you come," grunted Waters. "Plenty left."

"Hop Sing still cookin' for you?"

"Yeah."

"Ain't you ever goin' to get married?" chaffed Laramie.

"Shore," grunted the old man, chewing his pipe stem. "I just got to have time to decide what type of woman'd make me the best wife."

29

Laramie grinned. Waters was well past sixty, and had been giving that reply to chaffing about his matrimonial prospects as far back as Buck could remember.

Hop Sing remembered Laramie and greeted him warmly. The old Chinaman had cooked for Waters for many years. Laramie could trust him as far as he could trust Waters himself.

The old man sat gripping his cold pipe between his teeth as Laramie disposed of a steak, eggs, beans and potatoes and tamped it down with a man-sized chunk of apple pie.

"Yo're follerin' blind trails," he said slowly. "Mebbe I can help you."

"Maybe. Do you have any idea who the gent on the showy pinto might be?"

"Not many such paints in these parts. What'd the man look like?"

"Well, I didn't get a close range look at him, of course. From what I saw he looked to be short, thick-set, and he wore a short beard and a mustache so big it plumb ambushed his pan."

"Why, hell!" snorted Waters. "That's bound to be Mart Rawley! He rides a flashy pinto, and he's got the biggest set of whiskers in San Leon."

"Who's he?"

"Owns the Red Lode. Come here about six months ago and bought it off of old Charlie Ross."

"Well, that don't help none," growled Laramie, finishing his coffee and reaching for the makings. He paused suddenly, lighted match lifted. "Say, did this hombre ride up from Mexico?"

"He come in from the east. Of course, he could have come from Mexico, at that; he'd have circled the desert. Nobody but you Laramies ever hit straight across it. He ain't said he come from Mexico original; and he ain't said he ain't."

Laramie meditated in silence, and then asked: "What about this new gang that calls theirselves Laramies?"

"Plain coyotes," snarled the old man. "Us San Leon folks was just gittin' on our feet again after the wreck yore brothers made out of us, when this outfit hit the country. They've robbed and stole and looted till most of us are right back where we was six years ago. They've done more damage in a few weeks than yore brothers did in three years.

"I ain't been so bad hit as some, because I've got the toughest, straightest-shootin' crew of punchers in the county; but most of the cowmen around San Leon are mortgaged to the hilt, and stand to lose their outfits if they git looted any more. Ely Harrison--he's president of the bank now, since yore brothers killed old man Brown--Ely's been good about takin' mortgages and handin' out money, but he cain't go on doin' it forever."

"Does everybody figure they're the Laramies?"

"Why not? They send letters to the cowmen sayin' they'll wipe out their whole outfit if they don't deliver 'em so many hundred head of beef stock, and they sign them letters with the Laramie name. They're hidin' out in the Diablos like you all did; they's always the same number in the gang; and they can make a get-away through the desert, which nobody but the Laramies ever did.

"Of course, they wear masks, which the Laramies never did, but that's a minor item; customs change, so to speak. I'd have believed they was the genuine Laramies myself, only for a couple of reasons--one bein' you'd wrote me in your letter that you was the only Laramie left. You didn't give no details." The old man's voice was questioning.

"Man's reputation always follows him," grunted Buck. "A barroom gladiator got Jim. Hank got that gunfighter the next week, but was shot up so hisself he died. Tom joined the revolutionaries and the rurales cornered him in a dry wash. Took 'em ten hours and three dead men to get him. Luke--" He hesitated and scowled slightly.

"Luke was killed in a barroom brawl in Sante Maria, by a two-gunfighter called Killer Rawlins. They said Luke reached first, but Rawlins beat him to it. I don't know. Rawlins skipped that night. I've always believed that Luke got a dirty deal, some way. He was the best one of the boys. If I ever meet Rawlins--" Involuntarily his hand moved toward the worn butt of his Colt. Then he shrugged his shoulders, and said: "You said there was two reasons why you knowed these coyotes wasn't Laramies; what's t'other'n?"

"They work different," growled the old man. "Yore brothers was bad, but white men, just the same. They killed prompt, but they killed clean. These rats ain't content with just stealin' our stock. They burn down ranch houses and pizen water holes like a tribe of cussed Apaches. Jim Bannerman of the Lazy B didn't leave 'em two hundred of steers in a draw like they demanded in one of them letters. A couple of days later we found nothin' but smokin' ruins at the Lazy B, with Jim's body burned up inside and all his punchers dead or shot up."

Buck's face was gray beneath its tan. His fist knotted on the gunbutt.

"The devil!" he choked, in a voice little above a whisper. "And the Laramies are gettin' the blame! I thought my brothers dragged the name low--but these devils are haulin' it right down into hell. Joel Waters, listen to me! I come back here to pay back money my brothers stole from San Leon; I'm stayin' to pay a bigger debt. The desert's big, but it ain't big enough for a Laramie and the rats that wears his name. If I don't wipe that gang of rattlers off the earth they can have my name, because I won't need it no more."

"The Laramies owe a debt to San Leon," agreed old Joel, filling his pipe. "Cleanin' out that snake-den is the best way I know of payin' it."

33

Some time later Laramie rose at last and ground his cigarette butt under his heel.

"We've about talked out our wampum. From all I can see, everything points to this Mart Rawley bein' connected with the gang, somehow. He must have been the one that shot Bob Anders. He was ahead of the other fellows; they couldn't see him for a rise in the ground. They wouldn't have seen him shoot Anders. He might have been aimin' at me; or he might have just wanted Anders out of the way.

"Anyway, I'm headin' for the Diablos tonight. I know yo're willin' to hide me here, but you can help me more if nobody suspects yo're helpin' me, yet.

"I'm leavin' these saddle-bags with you. If I don't come back out of the Diablos, you'll know what to do with the money. So long."

They shook hands, and old Joel said: "So long, Buck. I'll take care of the money. If they git crowdin' you too close, duck back here. And if you need help in the hills, try to git word back to me. I can still draw a bead with a Winchester, and I've got a gang of hard-ridin' waddies to back my play."

"I ain't forgettin', Joel."

Laramie turned toward the door. Absorbed in his thoughts, he forgot for an instant that he was a hunted man, and relaxed his vigilance. As he stepped out onto the veranda he did not stop to think that he was thrown into bold relief by the light behind him.

As his boot-heel hit the porch yellow flame lanced the darkness and he heard the whine of a bullet that fanned him as it passed. He leapt back, slamming the door, wheeled, and halted in dismay to see Joel Waters sinking to the door. The old man, standing directly behind Laramie, had stopped the slug meant for his guest.

With his heart in his mouth Laramie dropped beside his friend. "Where'd it get you, Joel?" he choked.

"Low down, through the leg," grunted Waters, already sitting up and whipping his bandanna around his leg for a tourniquet. "Nothin' to worry about. You better git goin'."

Laramie took the bandanna and began knotting it tightly, ignoring a hail from without.

"Come out with yore hands up, Laramie!" a rough voice shouted. "You can't fight a whole posse. We got you cornered!"

"Beat it, Buck!" snapped Waters, pulling away his friend's hands. "They must have left their horses and sneaked up on foot. Sneak out the back way before they surround the house, fork yore cayuse and burn the breeze. That's Mart Rawley talkin', and I reckon it was him that shot. He aims to git you before you have time to ask questions or answer any. Even if you went out there with yore hands up, he'd kill you. Git goin', dern you!"

"All right!" Laramie jumped up as Hop Sing came out of the kitchen, almond eyes wide and a cleaver in his hand.

35

"Tell 'em I held a gun on you and made you feed me. T'ain't time for 'em to know we're friends, not yet."

The next instant he was gliding into the back part of the house and slipping through a window into the outer darkness. He heard somebody swearing at Rawley for firing before the rest had taken up their positions, and he heard other voices and noises that indicated the posse was scattering out to surround the house.

He ran for the blacksmith shop, and, groping in the dark, tightened the cinch on the sorrel and slipped on the bridle. He worked fast, but before Laramie could lead the horse outside he heard a jingle of spurs and the sound of footsteps.

Laramie swung into the saddle, ducked his head low to avoid the lintel of the door, and struck in the spurs. The sorrel hurtled through the door like a thunderbolt. A startled yell rang out, a man jumped frantically out of the way, tripped over his spurs and fell flat on his back, discharging his Winchester in the general direction of the Big Dipper. The sorrel and its rider went past him like a thundering shadow to be swallowed in the darkness. Wild yells answered the passionate blasphemy of the fallen man, and guns spurted red as their owners fired blindly after the receding hoof-beats. But before the possemen could untangle themselves from their bewilderment and find their mounts, the echoes of flying hoofs had died away and night hid the fugitive's trail. Buck Laramie was far away, riding to the Diablos.

CHAPTER IV:
SIDEWINDER RAMROD

Midnight found Laramie deep in the Diabios. He halted, tethered the sorrel, and spread his blankets at the foot of a low cliff. Night was not the time to venture further along the rock-strewn paths and treacherous precipices of the Diablos. He slept fitfully, his slumber disturbed by dreams of a girl kneeling beside a wounded man.

With the first gray of dawn he was riding familiar trails that would lead him to the cabin in the hidden canyon that he knew so well, the old hideout of his gang, where he believed he would find the new band which was terrorizing the country. The hideout had but one entrance--a rock-walled tunnel. How the fake gang could have learned of the place Laramie could not know.

The hideout was in a great bowl, on all sides of which rose walls of jumbled rock, impassable to a horseman. It was possible to climb the cliffs near the entrance of the tunnel, which, if the fake gang were following the customs of the real Laramies, would be guarded.

Half an hour after sunrise found him making his way on foot toward the canyon entrance. His horse he had left concealed among the rocks at a safe distance, and lariat in hand he crept along behind rocks and scrub growth toward the old river bed that formed the canyon. Presently, gazing through the underbrush that masked his approach, he saw, half hidden by a rock, a man in a tattered brown shirt who sat at the mouth of the canyon entrance, his hat pulled low over his eyes, and a Winchester across his knees.

Evidently a belief in the security of the hide-out made the sentry careless. Laramie had the drop on him; but to use his advantage incurred the possibility of a shot that would warn those inside the canyon and spoil his plans. So he retreated to a point where he would not be directly in the line of the guard's vision, if the man roused, and began working his way to a spot a few hundred yards to the left, where, as he knew of old, he could climb to the rim of the canyon.

In a few moments he had clambered up to a point from which he could glimpse the booted feet of the guard sticking from behind the rock. Laramie's flesh crawled at the thought of being picked off with a rifle bullet like a fly off a wall, if the guard looked his way.

But the boots did not move, he dislodged no stones large enough to make an alarming noise, and presently, panting and sweating, he heaved himself over the crest of the rim and lay on his belly gazing down into the canyon below him.

As he looked down into the bowl which had once been like a prison to him, bitterness of memory was mingled with a brief, sick longing for his dead brothers; after all, they were his brothers, and had been kind to him in their rough way.

The cabin below him had in no wise changed in the passing of the years. Smoke was pouring out of the chimney, and in the corral at the back, horses were milling about in an attempt to escape the ropes of two men who were seeking saddle mounts for the day.

Shaking out his lariat, Laramie crept along the canyon rim until he reached a spot where a stunted tree clung to the very edge. To this tree he made fast the rope, knotted it at intervals for handholds, and threw the other end over the cliff. It hung fifteen feet short of the bottom, but that was near enough.

As he went down it, with a knee hooked about the thin strand to take some of the strain off his hands, he grinned thinly as he remembered how he had used this descent long ago when he wanted to dodge Big Jim who was waiting at the entrance to give him a licking. His face hardened.

"Wish he was here with me now. We'd mop up these rats by ourselves."

Dangling at the end of the rope at arm's length he dropped, narrowly missing a heap of jagged rocks, and lit in the sand on his feet, going to his all-fours from the impact.

Bending low, sometimes on hands and knees, he headed circuitously for the cabin, keeping it between himself and the men in the corral. To his own wonderment he reached the cabin without hearing any alarm sounded. Maybe the occupants, if there were any in the canyon beside the men he had seen, had gone out the back way to the corral. He hoped so.

Cautiously he raised his head over a window sill and peered inside. He could see no one in the big room that constituted the front part of the cabin. Behind this room, he knew, were a bunk room and kitchen, and the back door was in the kitchen. There might be men in those backrooms; but he was willing to take the chance. He wanted to get in there and find a place where he could hide and spy.

The door was not locked; he pushed it open gently and stepped inside with a cat-like tread, Colt poked ahead of him.

"Stick 'em up!" Before he could complete the convulsive movement prompted by these unexpected words, he felt the barrel of a six-gun jammed hard against his backbone. He froze--opened his fingers and let his gun crash to the floor. There was nothing else for it.

The door to the bunkroom swung open and two men came out with drawn guns and triumphant leers on their unshaven faces. A third emerged from the kitchen. All were strangers to Laramie. He ventured to twist his head to look at his captor, and saw a big-boned, powerful man with a scarred face, grinning exultantly.

41

"That was easy," rumbled one of the others, a tall, heavily built ruffian whose figure looked somehow familiar. Laramie eyed him closely.

"So yo're 'Big Jim'," he said.

The big man scowled, but Scarface laughed.

"Yeah! With a mask on nobody can tell the difference. You ain't so slick, for a Laramie. I seen you sneakin' through the bresh ten minutes ago, and we been watchin' you ever since. I seen you aimed to come and make yoreself to home, so I app'inted myself a welcome committee of one--behind the door. You couldn't see me from the winder. Hey, you Joe!" he raised his voice pompously. "Gimme a piece of rope. Mister Laramie's goin' to stay with us for a spell."

Scarface shoved the bound Laramie into an old Morris chair that stood near the kitchen door. Laramie remembered that chair well; the brothers had brought it with them when they left their ranch home in the foothills.

He was trying to catch a nebulous memory that had something to do with that chair, when steps sounded in the bunkroom and "Jim" entered, accompanied by two others. One was an ordinary sort of criminal, slouchy, brutal faced and unshaven. The other was of an entirely different type. He was elderly and pale-faced, but that face was bleak and flinty. He did not seem range-bred like the others. Save for his high-heeled riding boots, he was dressed in town clothes, though the well-worn butt of a .45 jutted from a holster at his thigh.

Scarface hooked thumbs in belt and rocked back on his heels with an air of huge satisfaction. His big voice boomed in the cabin.

"Mister Harrison, I takes pleasure in makin' you acquainted with Mister Buck Laramie, the last of a family of honest horse-thieves, what's rode all the way from Mexico just to horn in on our play. And Mister Laramie, since you ain't long for this weary world, I'm likewise honored to interjuice you to Mister Ely Harrison, high man of our outfit and president of the Cattlemen's Bank of San Leon!"

Scarface had an eye for dramatics in his crude way. He bowed grotesquely, sweeping the floor with his Stetson and grinning gleefully at the astounded glare with which his prisoner greeted his introduction.

Harrison was less pleased.

"That tongue of yours wags too loose, Braxton," he snarled.

Scarface lapsed into injured silence, and Laramie found his tongue.

"Ely Harrison!" he said slowly. "Head of the gang--the pieces of this puzzle's beginnin' to fit. So you generously helps out the ranchers yore coyotes ruins--not forgettin' to grab a healthy mortgage while doin' it. And you was a hero and shot it out with the terrible bandits when they come for yore bank; only nobody gets hurt on either side."

Unconsciously he leaned further back in the Morris chair--and a lightning jolt of memory hit him just behind the ear. He stifled an involuntary grunt, and his fingers, hidden by his body from the eyes of his captors, began fumbling between the cushions of the chair.

He had remembered his jackknife, a beautiful implement, and the pride of his boyhood, stolen from him and hidden by his brother Tom, for a joke, a few days before they started for Mexico. Tom had forgotten all about it, and Buck had been too proud to beg him for it. But Tom had remembered, months later, in Mexico; had bought Buck a duplicate of the first knife, and told him that he had hidden the original between the cushions of the old Morris chair.

Laramie's heart almost choked him. It seemed too good to be true, this ace in the hole. Yet there was no reason to suppose anybody had found and removed the knife. His doubts were set at rest as his fingers encountered a smooth, hard object. It was not until that moment that he realized that Ely Harrison was speaking to him. He gathered his wits and concentrated on the man's rasping voice, while his hidden fingers fumbled with the knife, trying to open it.

"--damned unhealthy for a man to try to block my game," Harrison was saying harshly. "Why didn't you mind your own business?"

"How do you know I come here just to spoil yore game?" murmured Laramie absently.

"Then why did you come here?" Harrison's gaze was clouded with a sort of ferocious uncertainty. "Just how much did you know about our outfit before today? Did you know I was the leader of the gang?"

"Guess," suggested Laramie. The knife was open at last. He jammed the handle deep between the cushions and the chair-back, wedging it securely. The tendons along his wrists ached. It had been hard work, manipulating the knife with his cramped fingers, able to move just so far. His steady voice did not change in tone as he worked. "I was kind of ashamed of my name till I seen how much lower a man could go than my brothers ever went. They was hard men, but they was white, at least. Usin' my name to torture and murder behind my back plumb upsets me. Maybe I didn't come to San Leon just to spoil yore game; but maybe I decided to spoil it after I seen some of the hands you dealt."

"You'll spoil our game!" Harrison sneered. "Fat chance you've got of spoiling anybody's game. But you've got only yourself to blame. In another month I'd have owned every ranch within thirty miles of San Leon."

"So that's the idea, huh?" murmured Laramie, leaning forward to expectorate, and dragging his wrists hard across the knife-edge. He felt one strand part, and as he leaned back and repeated the movement, another gave way and the

45

edge bit into his flesh. If he could sever one more strand, he would make his break.

"Just how much did you know about our outfit before you came here?" demanded Harrison again, his persistence betraying his apprehension on that point. "How much did you tell Joel Waters?"

"None of yore derned business," Laramie snapped. His nerves getting on edge with the approach of the crisis.

"You'd better talk," snarled Harrison. "I've got men here who'd think nothing of shoving your feet in the fire to roast. Not that it matters. We're all set anyway. Got ready when we heard you'd ridden in. It just means we move tonight instead of a month later. But if you can prove to me that you haven't told anybody that I'm the real leader of the gang--well, we can carry out our original plans, and you'll save your life. We might even let you join the outfit."

"Join the--do you see any snake-scales on me?" flared Laramie, fiercely expanding his arm muscles. Another strand parted and the cords fell away from his wrists.

"Why you--" Murderous passion burst all bounds as Harrison lurched forward, his fist lifted. And Laramie shot from the chair like a steel spring released, catching them all flat-footed, paralyzed by the unexpectedness of the move.

One hand ripped Harrison's Colt from its scabbard. The other knotted into a fist that smashed hard in the banker's face and knocked him headlong into the midst of the men who stood behind him.

"Reach for the ceilin', you yellow-bellied polecats!" snarled Laramie, livid with fury and savage purpose; his cocked .45 menaced them all. "Reach! I'm dealin' this hand!"

CHAPTER V:
FIRST BLOOD

For an instant the scene held--then Scarface made a convulsive movement to duck behind the chair.

"Back up!" yelped Laramie, swinging his gun directly on him, and backing toward the door. But the tall outlaw who had impersonated Big Jim had recovered from the daze of his surprise. Even as Laramie's pistol muzzle moved in its short arc toward Braxton, the tall one's hand flashed like the stroke of a snake's head to his gun. It cleared leather just as Laramie's .45 banged.

Laramie felt hot wind fan his cheek, but the tall outlaw was sagging back and down, dying on his feet and grimly pulling trigger as he went. A hot welt burned across Laramie's left thigh, another slug ripped up splinters near his feet. Harrison had dived behind the Morris chair and Laramie's vengeful bullet smashed into the wall behind him.

It all happened so quickly that the others had barely unleathered their irons as he reached the threshold. He fired at Braxton, saw the scar-faced one drop his gun with a howl, saw "Big Jim" sprawl on the floor, done with impersonation and outlawry forever, and then he was slamming the door from the outside, wincing involuntarily as bullets smashed through the panels and whined about him.

His long legs flung him across the kitchen and he catapulted through the outer door. He collided head-on with the two men he had seen in the corral. All three went into the dust in a heap. One, even in falling, jammed his six-gun into Buck's belly and pulled trigger without stopping to see who it was. The hammer clicked on an empty chamber. Laramie, flesh crawling with the narrowness of his escape, crashed his gun barrel down on the other's head and sprang up, kicking free of the second man whom he recognized as Mart Rawley, he of the white sombrero and flashy pinto.

Rawley's gun had been knocked out of his hand in the collision. With a yelp the drygulcher scuttled around the corner of the cabin on hands and knees. Laramie did not stop for him. He had seen the one thing that might save him--a horse, saddled and bridled, tied to the corral fence.

He heard the furious stamp of boots behind him. Harrison's voice screamed commands as his enemies streamed out of the house and started pouring lead after him. Then a dozen long leaps carried him spraddle-legged to the startled mustang. With one movement he had ripped loose the tether and swung aboard. Over his shoulder he saw the men spreading out to head him off in the dash they expected him to make toward the head of the canyon. Then he wrenched the cayuse around and spurred through the corral gate which the outlaws had left half open.

49

In an instant Laramie was the center of a milling whirlpool of maddened horses as he yelled, fired in the air, and lashed them with the quirt hanging from the horn.

"Close the gate!" shrieked Harrison. One of the men ran to obey the command, but as he did, the snorting beasts came thundering through. Only a frantic leap backward saved him from being trampled to death under the maddened horses.

His companions yelped and ran for the protection of the cabin, firing blindly into the dust cloud that rose as the herd pounded past. Then Laramie was dashing through the scattering horde and drawing out of six-gun range, while his enemies howled like wolves behind him.

"Git along, cayuse!" yelled Laramie, drunk with the exhilaration of the hazard. "We done better'n I hoped. They got to round up their broncs before they hit my trail, and that's goin' to take time!"

Thought of the guard waiting at the canyon entrance did not sober him.

"Only way out is through the tunnel. Maybe he thinks the shootin' was just a family affair, and won't drill a gent ridin' from inside the canyon. Anyway, cayuse, we takes it on the run."

A Winchester banged from the mouth of the tunnel and the bullet cut the air past his ear.

"Pull up!" yelled a voice, but there was hesitancy in the tone. Doubtless the first shot had been a warning, and the sentry was puzzled. Laramie gave no heed; he ducked low and jammed in the spurs. He could see the rifle now, the blue muzzle resting on a boulder, and the ragged crown of a hat behind it. Even as he saw it, flame spurted from the blue ring. Laramie's horse stumbled in its headlong stride as lead ploughed through the fleshy part of its shoulder. That stumble saved Laramie's life for it lurched him out of the path of the next slug. His own six-gun roared.

The bullet smashed on the rock beside the rifle muzzle. Dazed and half-blinded by splinters of stone, the outlaw reeled back into the open, and fired without aim. The Winchester flamed almost in Laramie's face. Then his answering slug knocked the guard down as if he had been hit with a hammer. The Winchester flew out of his hands as he rolled on the ground. Laramie jerked the half-frantic mustang back on its haunches and dived out of the saddle to grab for the rifle.

"Damn!" It had struck the sharp edge of a rock as it fell. The lock was bent and the weapon useless. He cast it aside disgustedly, wheeled toward his horse, and then halted to stare down at the man he had shot. The fellow had hauled himself to a half-sitting position. His face was pallid, and blood oozed from a round hole in his shirt bosom. He was dying. Sudden revulsion shook Laramie as he saw his victim was hardly more than a boy. His berserk excitement faded.

"Laramie!" gasped the youth. "You must be Buck Laramie!"

"Yeah," admitted Laramie. "Anything--anything I can do?"

The boy grinned in spite of his pain.

"Thought so. Nobody but a Laramie could ride so reckless and shoot so straight. Seems funny--bein' plugged by a Laramie after worshippin' 'em most of my life."

"What?" ejaculated Laramie.

"I always wanted to be like 'em," gasped the youth. "Nobody could ride and shoot and fight like them. That's why I j'ined up with these polecats. They said they was startin' up a gang that was to be just like the Laramies. But they ain't; they're a passel of dirty coyotes. Once I started in with 'em, though, I had to stick."

Laramie said nothing. It was appalling to think that a young life had been so warped, and at last destroyed, by the evil example of his brothers.

"You better go and raise a posse if yo're aimin' to git them rats," the boy said. "They's goin' to be hell to pay tonight."

"How's that?" questioned Laramie, remembering Harrison's remarks about something planned for the night.

"You got 'em scared," murmured the boy. "Harrison's scared you might have told Joel Waters he was boss-man of the gang. That's why he come here last night. They'd aimed to keep stealin' for another month. Old Harrison woulda had most all the ranches around here by then, foreclosin' mortgages.

"When Mart Rawley failed to git you, old Harrison sent out word for the boys to git together here today. They figgered on huntin' you down, if the posse from San Leon hadn't already got you. If they found out you didn't know nothin' and hadn't told nobody nothin', they just aimed to kill you and go on like they'd planned from the first. But if they didn't git you, or found you'd talked, they aimed to make their big cleanup tonight, and then ride."

"What's that?" asked Laramie.

"They're goin' down tonight and burn Joel Waters' ranch buildings, and the sheriff's, and some of the other big ones. They'll drive all the cattle off to Mexico over the old Laramie trail. Then old Harrison'll divide the loot and the gang will scatter. If he finds you ain't spilled the works about him bein' the top man, he'll stay on in San Leon. That was his idee from the start--ruin the ranchers, buy up their outfits cheap and be king of San Leon."

"How many men's he got?"

"'Tween twenty-five and thirty," panted the youth. He was going fast. He choked, and a trickle of blood began at the corner of his mouth. "I ought not to be squealin', maybe; t'ain't the Laramie way. But I wouldn't to nobody but a Laramie. You didn't see near all of 'em. Two died on the way back from San Leon, yesterday. They left 'em out in the desert. The rest ain't got back from drivin' cattle to Mexico, but they'll be on hand by noon today."

Laramie was silent, reckoning on the force he could put in the field. Waters' punchers were all he could be sure of--six or seven men at the most, not counting the wounded Waters. The odds were stacking up.

"Got a smoke?" the youth asked weakly. Laramie rolled a cigarette, placed it between the blue lips and held a match. Looking back down the canyon, Laramie saw men saddling mounts. Precious time was passing, but he was loath to leave the dying lad.

"Get goin'," muttered the boy uneasily. "You got a tough job ahead of you--honest men and thieves both agen you--but I'm bettin' on the Laramies--the real ones--" He seemed wandering in his mind. He began to sing in a ghastly whisper the song that Laramie could never hear without a shudder.

"When Brady died they planted him deep,
Put a bottle of whisky at his head and feet.
Folded his arms across his breast.
And said: 'King Brady's gone to his rest!'"

The crimson trickle became a sudden spurt; the youth's voice trailed into silence. The cigarette slipped from his lips. He went limp and lay still, through forever with the wolf-trail.

Laramie rose heavily and groped for his horse, trembling in the shade of the rock. He tore the blanket rolled behind the saddle and covered the still figure. Another debt to be marked up against the Laramies.

He swung aboard and galloped through the tunnel to where his own horse was waiting--a faster mount than the cayuse he was riding. As he shifted mounts he heard shouts behind him, knew that his pursuers had halted at the body, knew the halt would be brief.

Without looking back, he hit the straightest trail he knew that led toward the ranch of Joel Waters.

CHAPTER VI:
"STRING HIM UP"

It was nearly noon when Laramie pulled up his sweating bronc at the porch of the Boxed W ranch house. There were no punchers in sight. Hop Sing opened the door.

"Where's Waters?" rapped out Laramie.

"Solly!" Hop Sing beamed on the younger man. "He gone to town to see doctluh and get leg fixed. Slim Jones dlive him in in buckbload. He be back tonight."

"Damn!" groaned Laramie. He saw his plan being knocked into a cocked hat. That plan had been to lead a band of men straight to the outlaws' hide-out and bottle them up in their stronghold before they could scatter out over the range in their planned raid. The Boxed W punchers would not follow a stranger without their boss's orders, and only Waters could convince the bellicose citizens of San Leon that Laramie was on the level. Time was flying, and every minute counted.

There was only one risky course left open. He swung on his tiring horse and reined away on the road for San Leon.

He met no one on the road, for which he was thankful. When he drew up on the outskirts of the town his horse was drawing laboring breaths. He knew the animal would be useless in case he had to dust out of town with a posse on his heels.

Laramie knew of a back alley that led to the doctor's office, and by which he hoped to make it unseen. He dismounted and headed down the alley, leading the gelding by the reins.

He sighted the little adobe shack where the town's one physician lived and worked, when a jingle of spurs behind him caused him to jerk his head in time to see a man passing the end of the alley. It was Mart Rawley, and Laramie ducked behind his horse, cursing his luck. Rawley must have been prowling around the town, expecting him, and watching for him. His yell instantly split the lazy silence.

"Laramie!" howled Rawley. "Laramie's back! Hey, Bill! Lon! Joe! Everybody! Laramie's in town again! This way!"

Laramie forked his mustang and spurred it into a lumbering run for the main street. Lead was singing down the alley as Laramie burst into Main Street, and saw Joel Waters sitting in a chair on the porch of the doctor's shack.

"Get all the men you can rustle and head for the Diablos!" he yelled at the astonished ranchman. "I'll leave a trail for you to follow. I found the gang at the old hide-out--and they're comin' out tonight for a big cleanup!"

Then he was off again, his clattering hoofs drowning Waters' voice as he shouted after the rider. Men were yelling and .45s banging. Ahorse and afoot they came at him, shooting as they ran. The dull, terrifying mob-roar rose, pierced with yells of: "String him up!" "He shot Bob Anders in the back!"

His way to open country was blocked, and his horse was exhausted. With a snarl Laramie wheeled and rode to the right for a narrow alley that did not seem to be blocked. It led between two buildings to a side-street, and was not wide enough for a horse to pass through. Maybe that was the reason it had been left unguarded. Laramie reached it, threw himself from his saddle and dived into the narrow mouth.

For an instant his mount, standing with drooping head in the opening, masked his master from bullets, though Laramie had not intended sacrificing his horse for his own hide. Laramie had run half the length of the alley before someone reached out gingerly, grasped the reins and jerked the horse away. Laramie half turned, without pausing in his run, and fired high and harmlessly back down the alley. The whistle of lead kept the alley clear until he bolted out the other end.

There, blocking his way in the side, street, stood a figure beside a black racing horse. Laramie's gun came up--then he stopped short, mouth open in amazement. It was Judy Anders who stood beside the black horse.

Before he could speak she sprang forward and thrust the reins in his hand.

"Take him and go! He's fast!"

"Why--what?" Laramie sputtered, his thinking processes in a muddle. The mere sight of Judy Anders had that effect upon him. Hope flamed in him. Did her helping him mean--then reason returned and he took the gift the gods had given him without stopping for question. As he grabbed the horn and swung up he managed: "I sure thank you kindly, miss--"

"Don't thank me," Judy Anders retorted curtly; her color was high, but her red lips were sulky. "You're a Laramie and ought to be hung, but you fought beside Bob yesterday when he needed help. The Anderses pay their debts. Will you go?"

A nervous stamp of her little foot emphasized the request. The advice was good. Three of the townsmen appeared with lifted guns around a corner of a nearby building. They hesitated as they saw the girl near him, but began maneuvering for a clear shot at him without endangering her.

"See Joel Waters, at the doctor's office!" he yelled to her, and was off for the open country, riding like an Apache, and not at all sure that she understood him. Men howled and guns crashed behind him, and maddened citizens ran cursing for their mounts, too crazy-mad to notice the girl who shrieked vainly at them, unheeding her waving arms.

"Stop! Stop! Wait! Listen to me!" Deaf to her cries they streamed past her, ahorse and afoot, and burst out into the open. The mounted men spurred their horses savagely after the figure that was swiftly dwindling in the distance.

Judy dashed aside an angry tear and declaimed her opinion of men in general, and the citizens of San Leon in particular, in terms more expressive than lady-like.

"What's the matter?" It was Joel Waters, limping out of the alley, supported by the doctor. The old man seemed stunned by the rapidity of events. "What in the devil's all this mean? Where's Buck?"

She pointed. "There he goes, with all the idiots in San Leon after him."

"Not all the idiots," Waters corrected. "I'm still here. Dern it, the boy must be crazy, comin' here. I yelled myself deef at them fools, but they wouldn't listen--"

"They wouldn't listen to me, either!" cried Judy despairingly. "But they won't catch him--ever, on that black of mine. And maybe when they come limping back, they'll be cooled down enough to hear the truth. If they won't listen to me, they will to Bob!"

"To Bob?" exclaimed the doctor. "Has he come out of his daze? I was just getting ready to come over and see him again, when Joel came in for his leg to be dressed."

"Bob came out of it just a little while ago. He told me it wasn't Laramie who shot him. He's still groggy and uncertain as to just what happened. He doesn't know who it was who shot him, but he knows it wasn't Buck Laramie.

The last thing he remembers was Laramie running some little distance ahead of him. The bullet came from behind. He thinks a stray slug from the men behind them hit him."

"I don't believe it was a stray," grunted Waters, his eyes beginning to glitter. "I got a dern good idee who shot Bob. I'm goin' to talk--"

"Better not bother Bob too much right now," interrupted the doctor "I'll go over there--"

"Better go in a hurry if you want to catch Bob at home," the girl said grimly. "He was pulling on his boots and yelling for our cook to bring him his gun-belt when I left!"

"What? Why, he musn't get up yet!" The doctor transferred Waters' arm from his shoulder to that of the girl, and hurried away toward the house where Bob Anders was supposed to be convalescing.

"Why did Buck come back here?" Judy wailed to Waters.

"From what he hollered at me as he lighted past, I reckon he's found somethin' up in the Diablos. He come for help. Probably went to my ranch first, and findin' me not there, risked his neck comin' on here. Said send men after him, to foller signs he'd leave. I relayed that there information on to Slim Jones, my foreman. Doc lent Slim a horse, and Slim's high-tailin' it for the Boxed W right now to round up my waddies and hit the trail. As soon as these San Leon snake-hunters has ruint their cayuses chasin' that black streak of light you give Buck, they'll be pullin' back into town. This time, I bet they'll listen."

"I'm glad he didn't shoot Bob," she murmured. "But why--why did he come back here in the first place?"

"He come to pay a debt he figgered he owed on behalf of his no-account brothers. His saddle bags is full of gold he aims to give back to the citizens of this here ongrateful town. What's the matter?"

For his fair companion had uttered a startled exclamation.

"N-nothing, only--only I didn't know it was that way! Then Buck never robbed or stole, like his brothers?"

"Course he didn't!" snapped the old man irascibly. "Think I'd kept on bein' his friend all his life, if he had? Buck ain't to blame for what his brothers did. He's straight and he's always been straight."

"But he was with them, when--when--"

"I know." Waters' voice was gentler. "But he didn't shoot yore dad. That was Luke. And Buck was with 'em only because they made him. He wasn't nothin' but a kid."

She did not reply and old Waters, noting the soft, new light glowing in her eyes, the faint, wistful smile that curved her lips, wisely said nothing.

In the meantime the subject of their discussion was proving the worth of the sleek piece of horseflesh under him. He grinned as he saw the distance between him and his pursuers widen, thrilled to the marvel of the horse between his knees as any good horseman would. In half an hour he could no longer see the men who hunted him.

He pulled the black to an easier, swinging gait that would eat up the miles for long hours on end, and headed for the Diablos. But the desperate move he was making was not dominating his thoughts. He was mulling over a new puzzle; the problem of why Judy Anders had come to his aid. Considering her parting words, she didn't have much use for him. If Bob had survived his wound, and asserted Laramie's innocence, why were the citizens so hot for his blood? If not--would Judy Anders willingly aid a man she thought shot her brother? He thrilled at the memory of her, standing there with the horse that saved his life. If only he weren't a Laramie--How beautiful she was.

CHAPTER VII:
BOTTLED UP

A good three hours before sundown Laramie was in the foothills of the Diablos. In another hour, by dint of reckless riding over trails that were inches in width, which even he ordinarily would have shunned, he came in sight of the entrance to the hide-out. He had left signs farther down the trail to indicate, not the way he had come, but the best way for Waters' punchers to follow him.

Once more he dismounted some distance from the tunnel and stole cautiously forward. There would be a new sentry at the entrance, and Laramie's first job must be to dispose of him silently.

He was halfway to the tunnel when he glimpsed the guard, sitting several yards from the mouth, near a clump of bushes. It was the scar-faced fellow Harrison had called Braxton, and he seemed wide-awake.

Falling back on Indian tactics, acquired from the Yaquis in Mexico, Laramie began a stealthy, and necessarily slow, advance on the guard, swinging in a circle that would bring him behind the man. He crept up to within a dozen feet.

Braxton was getting restless. He shifted his position, craning his neck as he stared suspiciously about him. Laramie believed he had heard, but not yet located, faint sounds made in Laramie's progress. In another instant he would turn his head and stare full at the bushes which afforded the attacker scanty cover.

Gathering a handful of pebbles, Laramie rose stealthily to his knees and threw them over the guard's head. They hit with a loud clatter some yards beyond the man. Braxton started to his feet with an oath. He glared in the direction of the sound with his Winchester half lifted, neck craned. At the same instant Laramie leaped for him with his six-gun raised like a club.

Scarface wheeled, and his eyes flared in amazement. He jerked the rifle around, but Laramie struck it aside with his left hand, and brought down his pistol barrel crushingly on the man's head. Braxton went to his knees like a felled ox; slumped full-length and lay still.

Laramie ripped off belts and neckerchief from the senseless figure; bound and gagged his captive securely. He appropriated his pistol, rifle and spare cartridges, then dragged him away from the tunnel mouth and shoved him in among a cluster of rocks and bushes, effectually concealing him from the casual glance.

"Won the first trick, by thunder!" grunted Laramie. "And now for the next deal."

The success of that deal depended on whether or not all the outlaws of Harrison's band were in the hide-out. Mart Rawley was probably outside, yet; maybe still back in San

Leon. But Laramie knew he must take the chance that all the other outlaws were inside.

He glanced up to a ledge overhanging the tunnel mouth, where stood precariously balanced the huge boulder which had given him his idea for bottling up the canyon.

"Cork for my bottle!" muttered Laramie. "All I need now's a lever."

A broken tree limb sufficed for that, and a few moments later he had climbed to the ledge and was at work on the boulder. A moment's panic assailed him as he feared its base was too deeply imbedded for him to move it. But under his fierce efforts he felt the great mass give at last. A few minutes more of back-breaking effort, another heave that made the veins bulge on his temples--and the boulder started toppling, crashed over the ledge and thundered down into the tunnel entrance. It jammed there, almost filling the space.

He swarmed down the wall and began wedging smaller rocks and brush in the apertures between the boulder and the tunnel sides. The only way his enemies could get out now was by climbing the canyon walls, a feat he considered practically impossible, or by laboriously picking out the stones he had jammed in place, and squeezing a way through a hole between the boulder and the tunnel wall. And neither method would be a cinch, with a resolute cowpuncher slinging lead at everything that moved.

Laramie estimated that his whole task had taken about half an hour. Slinging Braxton's rifle over his shoulder he clambered up the cliffs. At the spot on the canyon rim where he had spied upon the hide-out that morning, he forted himself by the simple procedure of crouching behind a fair-sized rock, with the Winchester and pistols handy at his elbows. He had scarcely taken his position when he saw a mob of riders breaking away from the corral behind the cabin. As he had figured, the gang was getting away to an early start for its activities of the night.

He counted twenty-five of them; and the very sun that glinted on polished gun hammers and silver conchas seemed to reflect violence and evil deeds.

"Four hundred yards," muttered Laramie, squinting along the blue rifle barrel. "Three fifty--three hundred--now I opens the ball!"

At the ping of the shot dust spurted in front of the horses' hoofs, and the riders scattered like quail, with startled yells.

"Drop them shootin' irons and hi'st yore hands!" roared Laramie. "Tunnel's corked up and you can't get out!"

His answer came in a vengeful hail of bullets, spattering along the canyon rim for yards in either direction. He had not expected any other reply. His shout had been more for rhetorical effect than anything else. But there was nothing theatrical about his second shot, which knocked a man out of his saddle. The fellow never moved after he hit the ground.

The outlaws converged toward the tunnel entrance, firing as they rode, aiming at Laramie's aerie, which they had finally located. Laramie replied in kind. A mustang smitten by a slug meant for his rider rolled to the ground and broke his rider's leg under him. A squat raider howled profanely as a slug ploughed through his breast muscles.

Then half a dozen men in the lead jammed into the tunnel and found that Laramie had informed them truthfully. Their yells reached a crescendo of fury. The others slid from their horses and took cover behind the rocks that littered the edges of the canyon, dragging the wounded men with them.

From a rush and a dash the fight settled to a slow, deadly grind, with nobody taking any rash chances. Having located his tiny fort, they concentrated their fire on the spot of the rim he occupied. A storm of bullets drove him to cover behind the breastworks, and became exceedingly irksome.

He had not seen either Rawley or Harrison. Rawley, he hoped, was still in San Leon, but the absence of Harrison worried him. Had he, too, gone to San Leon? If so, there was every chance that he might get clean away, even if his band was wiped out. There was another chance, that he or Rawley, or both of them, might return to the hide-out and attack him from the rear. He cursed himself for not having divulged the true identity of the gang's leader to Judy Anders; but he always seemed addled when talking to her.

The ammunition supply of the outlaws seemed inexhaustible. He knew at least six men were in the tunnel, and he heard them cursing and shouting, their voices muffled. He found himself confronted by a quandary that seemed to admit of no solution. If he did not discourage them, they would be breaking through the blocked tunnel and potting him from the rear. But to affect this discouragement meant leaving his point of vantage, and giving the men below a chance to climb the canyon wall. He did not believe this could be done, but he did not know what additions to the fortress had been made by the new occupants. They might have chiseled out handholds at some point on the wall. Well, he'd have to look at the tunnel.

"Six-guns against rifles, if this keeps up much longer," he muttered, working his way over the ledges. "Cartridges most gone. Why the devil don't Joel's men show up? I can't keep these hombres hemmed up forever--damn!"

His arm thrust his six-gun out as he yelped. Stones and brush had been worked out at one place in the tunnel-mouth, and the head and shoulders of a man appeared. At the crash of Laramie's Colt the fellow howled and vanished. Laramie crouched, glaring; they would try it again, soon. If he was not there to give them lead-argument, the whole gang would be squeezing out of the tunnel in no time.

He could not get back to the rim, and leave the tunnel unguarded; yet there was always the possibility of somebody climbing the canyon wall.

Had he but known it, his fears were justified. For while he crouched on the ledge, glaring down at the tunnel-mouth, down in the canyon a man was wriggling toward a certain point of the cliff, where his keen eyes had discerned something dangling. He had discovered Laramie's rope, hanging from the stunted tree on the rim. Cautiously he lifted himself out of the tall grass, ready to duck back in an instant, then as no shot came from the canyon rim, he scuttled like a rabbit toward the wall.

Kicking off his boots and slinging his rifle on his back, he began swarming, ape-like, up the almost sheer wall. His outstretched arm grasped the lower end of the rope, just as the others in the canyon saw what he was doing, and opened a furious fire on the rim to cover his activities. The outlaw on the rope swore luridly, and went up with amazing agility, his flesh crawling with the momentary expectation of a bullet in his back.

The renewed firing had just the effect on Laramie that the climber had feared it would have--it drew him back to his breastwork. It was not until he was crouching behind his breastwork that it occurred to him that the volleys might have been intended to draw him away from the tunnel. So he spared only a limited glance over the rocks, for the bullets were winging so close that he dared not lift his head high. He did not see the man on the rope cover the last few feet in a scrambling rush, and haul himself over the rim, unslinging his rifle as he did so.

Laramie turned and headed back for the ledge whence he could see the opening. And as he did so, he brought himself into full view of the outlaw who was standing upright on the rim, by the stunted tree.

The whip-like crack of his Winchester reached Laramie an instant after he felt a numbing impact in his left shoulder. The shock of the blow knocked him off his feet, and his head hit hard against a rock. Even as he fell he heard the crashing of brush down the trail, and his last, hopeless thought was that Rawley and Harrison were returning. Then the impact of his head against the rock knocked all thought into a stunned blank.

CHAPTER VIII:
BOOT HILL TALK

An outlaw came scrambling out of the tunnel with desperate haste, followed by another and another. One crouched, rifle in hand, glaring up at the wall, while the others tore away the smaller stones, and aided by those inside, rolled the boulder out of the entrance. Three men ran out of the tunnel and joined them.

Their firing roused Buck Laramie. He blinked and glared, then oriented himself. He saw five riders sweeping toward the tunnel, and six outlaws who had rushed out while he was unconscious, falling back into it for shelter; and he recognized the leader of the newcomers as Slim Jones, Joel Waters' foreman. The old man had not failed him.

"Take cover, you fools!" Laramie yelled wildly, unheard in the din.

But the reckless punchers came straight on and ran into a blast of lead poured from the tunnel mouth into which the outlaws had disappeared. One of the waddies saved his life by a leap from the saddle as his horse fell with a bullet through its brain, and another man threw wide his arms and pitched on his head, dead before he hit the pebbles.

Then only did Slim and his wild crew swerve their horses out of line and fall back to cover. Laramie remembered the slug that had felled him, and turned to scan the canyon rim. He saw the man by the stunted tree then; the fellow was helping one of his companions up the same route he had taken, and evidently thought that his shot had settled Laramie, as he was making no effort at concealment. Laramie lifted his rifle and pulled the trigger--and the hammer fell with an empty click. He had no more rifle cartridges. Below him the punchers were futilely firing at the tunnel entrance, and the outlaws within were wisely holding their fire until they could see something to shoot at.

Laramie crawled along a few feet to put himself out of range of the rifleman on the rim, then shouted: "Slim! Swing wide of that trail and come up here with yore men!"

He was understood, for presently Slim and the three surviving punchers came crawling over the tangle of rocks, having necessarily abandoned their horses.

"'Bout time you was gettin' here," grunted Laramie. "Gimme some .30-30s."

A handful of cartridges were shoved into his eager fingers.

"We come as soon as we could," said Slim. "Had to ride to the ranch to round up these snake-hunters."

"Where's Waters?"

"I left him in San Leon, cussin' a blue streak because he couldn't get nobody to listen to him. Folks got no more sense'n cattle; just as easy to stampede and as hard to git millin' once they bust loose."

"What about Bob Anders?"

"Doctor said he was just creased; was just fixin' to go over there when me and Joel come into town and he had to wait and dress Joel's leg. Hadn't come to hisself, last time the doc was there."

Laramie breathed a sigh of relief. At least Bob Anders was going to live, even if he hadn't been able to name the man who shot him. Soon Judy would know the truth. Laramie snapped into action.

"Unless Waters sends us more men, we're licked. Tunnel's cleared and men climbin' the cliff."

"You're shot!" Jones pointed to Laramie's shirt shoulder, soaked with blood.

"Forget it!" snapped Laramie. "Well, gimme that bandanna--" and while he knotted it into a crude bandage, he talked rapidly. "Three of you hombres stay here and watch that tunnel. Don't let nobody out, d'you hear? Me and Slim are goin' to circle around and argy with the gents climbin' the cliffs. Come on, Slim."

It was rough climbing, and Laramie's shoulder burned like fire, with a dull throbbing that told him the lead was pressing near a bone. But he set his teeth and crawled over the rough rocks, keeping out of sight of the men in the canyon below, until they had reached a point beyond his tiny fort on the rim, and that much closer to the stunted tree.

They had kept below the crest and had not been sighted by the outlaws on the rim, who had been engrossed in knotting a second rope, brought up by the second man, to the end of the lariat tied to the tree. This had been dropped down the wall again, and now another outlaw was hanging to the rope and being drawn straight up the cliff like a water bucket by his two friends above.

Slim and Laramie fired almost simultaneously. Slim's bullet burned the fingers of the man clinging to the lariat. He howled and let go the rope and fell fifteen feet to the canyon floor. Laramie winged one of the men on the cliff, but it did not affect his speed as he raced after his companion in a flight for cover. Bullets whizzed up from the canyon as the men below spotted Laramie and his companion. They ducked back, but relentlessly piled lead after the men fleeing along the rim of the cliff.

These worthies made no attempt to make a stand. They knew the lone defender had received reinforcements and they were not stopping to learn in what force. Laramie and Slim caught fleeting glimpses of the fugitives as they headed out through the hills.

"Let 'em go," grunted Laramie. "Be no more trouble from that quarter, and I bet them rannies won't try to climb that rope no more. Come on; I hear guns talkin' back at the tunnel."

Laramie and his companion reached the punchers on the ledge in time to see three horsemen streaking it down the trail, with lead humming after them. Three more figures lay sprawled about the mouth of the tunnel.

"They busted out on horseback," grunted one of the men, kneeling and aiming after the fleeing men. "Come so fast we couldn't stop 'em all--uh."

His shot punctuated his remarks, and one of the fleeing horsemen swayed in his saddle. One of the others seemed to be wounded, as the three ducked into the trees and out of sight.

"Three more hit the trail," grunted Slim.

"Not them," predicted Laramie. "They was bound to see us--know they ain't but five of us. They won't go far; they'll be sneakin' back to pot us in the back when their pards start bustin' out again."

"No racket in the tunnel now."

"They're layin' low for a spell. Too damn risky now. They didn't have but six horses in the tunnel. They got to catch more and bring 'em to the tunnel before they can make the rush.

"They'll wait till dark, and then we can't stop 'em from gettin' their cayuses into the tunnel. We can't stop 'em from tearin' out at this end, neither, unless we got more men.

Slim, climb back up on the rim and lay down behind them rocks I stacked up. Watch that rope so nobody climbs it; we got to cut that, soon's it gets dark. And don't let no horses be brought into the tunnel, if you can help it."

Slim crawled away, and a few moments later his rifle began banging, and he yelled wrathfully: "They're already at it!"

"Listen!" ejaculated Laramie suddenly.

Down the trail, out of sight among the trees sounded a thundering of hoofs, yells and shots.

The shots ceased, then after a pause, the hoofs swept on, and a crowd of men burst into view.

"Yippee!" whooped one of the punchers bounding into the air and swinging his hat. "Reinforcements, b'golly! It's a regular army!"

"Looks like all San Leon was there!" bellowed another. "Hey, boys, don't git in line with that tunnel mouth! Spread out along the trail--who's them three fellers they got tied to their saddles?"

"The three snakes that broke loose from the tunnel!" yelped the third cowboy. "They scooped 'em in as they come! Looks like everybody's there. There's Charlie Ross, and Jim Watkins, the mayor, and Lon Evans, Mart Rawley's bartender--reckon he didn't know his boss was a crook--and by golly, look who's leadin' 'em!"

"Bob Anders!" ejaculated Laramie, staring at the pale-faced, but erect figure who, with bandaged head, rode ahead of the thirty or forty men who came clattering up the trail and swung wide through the brush to avoid the grim tunnel mouth. Anders saw him and waved his hand, and a deep yell of approbation rose from the men behind the sheriff. Laramie sighed deeply. A few hours ago these same men wanted to hang him.

Rifles were spitting from the tunnel, and the riders swung from their horses and began to take up positions on each side of the trail, as Anders took in the situation at a glance and snapped his orders. Rifles began to speak in answer to the shots of the outlaws. Laramie came clambering down the cliff to grasp Anders' outstretched hand.

"I came to just about the time you hit town today, Laramie," he said. "Was just tellin' Judy it couldn't been you that shot me, when all that hell busted loose and Judy run to help you out if she could. Time I could get my clothes on, and out-argy the doctor, and get on the streets, you was gone with these addle-heads chasin' you. We had to wait till they give up the chase and come back, and then me and Judy and Joel Waters lit into 'em. Time we got through talkin' they was plumb whipped down and achin' to take a hand in yore game."

"I owe you all a lot, especially your sister. Where's Rawley?" Laramie asked.

"We thought he was with us when we lit out after you," the sheriff answered. "But when we started back we missed him."

"Look out!" yelled Slim on the rim above them, pumping lead frantically. "They're rushin' for the tunnel on horses! Blame it, why ain't somebody up here with me? I can't stop 'em all--"

Evidently the gang inside the canyon had been whipped to desperation by the arrival of the reinforcements, for they came thundering through the tunnel laying down a barrage of lead as they came. It was sheer madness. They ran full into a blast of lead that piled screaming horses and writhing men in a red shambles. The survivors staggered back into the tunnel.

Struck by a sudden thought, Laramie groped among the bushes and hauled out the guard, Braxton, still bound and gagged. The fellow was conscious and glared balefully at his captor. Laramie tore the gag off, and demanded: "Where's Harrison and Rawley?"

"Rawley rode for San Leon after you got away from us this mornin'," growled Braxton sullenly. "Harrison's gone, got scared and pulled out. I dunno where he went."

"Yo're lyin'," accused Laramie.

"What'd you ast me for, if you know so much?" sneered Braxton, and lapsed in stubborn, hill-country silence, which

Laramie knew nothing would break, so long as the man chose to hold his tongue.

"You mean Harrison's in on this, Buck?" the sheriff exclaimed. "Joel told me about Rawley."

"In on it?" Laramie laughed grimly. "Harrison is the kingpin, and Rawley is his chief sidewinder, I ain't seen neither Harrison nor Rawley since I got here. Be just like them rats to double-cross their own men, and run off with the loot they've already got.

"But we still got this nest to clean out, and here's my idea. Them that's still alive in the canyon are denned up in or near the tunnel. Nobody nigh the cabin. If four or five of us can hole up in there, we'll have 'em from both sides. We'll tie some lariats together, and some of us will go down the walls and get in the cabin. We'll scatter men along the rim to see none of 'em climb out, and we'll leave plenty men here to hold the tunnel if they try that again--which they will, as soon as it begins to get dark, if we don't scuttle 'em first."

"You ought a been a general, cowboy. Me and Slim and a couple of my Bar X boys'll go for the cabin. You better stay here; yore shoulder ain't fit for tight-rope work and such."

"She's my hand," growled Laramie. "I started dealin' her and I aim to set in till the last pot's raked in."

"Yo're the dealer," acquiesced Anders. "Let's go."

Ten minutes later found the party of five clustered on the canyon rim. The sun had not yet set beyond the peaks, but the canyon below was in shadow. The spot Laramie had chosen for descent was some distance beyond the stunted tree. The rim there was higher, the wall even more precipitous. It had the advantage, however, of an outjut of rock that would partially serve to mask the descent of a man on a lariat from the view of the men lurking about the head of the canyon.

If anyone saw the descent of the five invaders, there was no sign to show they had been discovered. Man after man they slid down the dangling rope and crouched at the foot, Winchesters ready. Laramie came last, clinging with one hand and gritting his teeth against the pain of his wounded shoulder. Then began the advance on the cabin.

That slow, tortuous crawl across the canyon floor seemed endless. Laramie counted the seconds, fearful that they would be seen, fearful that night would shut down before they were forted. The western rim of the canyon seemed crested with golden fire, contrasting with the blue shadows floating beneath it. He sighed gustily as they reached their goal, with still enough light for their purpose.

The cabin doors were shut, the windows closely shuttered.

"Let's go!" Anders had one hand on the door, drawn Colt in the other.

"Wait," grunted Laramie. "I stuck my head into a loop here once already today. You all stay here while I take a pasear around to the back and look things over from that side. Don't go in till you hear me holler."

Then Laramie was sneaking around the cabin, Indian-fashion, gun in hand. He was little more than half the distance to the back when he was paralyzed to hear a voice inside the cabin call out: "All clear!"

Before he could move or shout a warning, he heard Anders answer: "Comin', Buck!" Then the front door slammed, and there was the sound of a sliding bolt, a yell of dismay from the Bar X men. With sick fury Laramie realized that somebody lurking inside the cabin had heard him giving his instructions and imitated his voice to trick the sheriff into entering. Confirmation came instantly, in a familiar voice--the voice of Ely Harrison!

"Now we can make terms, gentlemen!" shouted the banker, his voice rasping with ferocious exultation. "We've got your sheriff in a wolf-trap with hot lead teeth! You can give us road-belts to Mexico, or he'll be deader than hell in three minutes!"

CHAPTER IX:
KILLER UNMASKED

Laramie was charging for the rear of the house before the triumphant shout ended. Anders would never agree to buying freedom for that gang to save his own life; and Laramie knew that whatever truce might be agreed upon, Harrison would never let the sheriff live.

The same thought motivated the savage attack of Slim Jones and the Bar X men on the front door; but that door happened to be of unusual strength. Nothing short of a log battering ram could smash it. The rear door was of ordinary thin paneling.

Bracing his good right shoulder to the shock, Laramie rammed his full charging weight against the rear door. It crashed inward and he catapulted into the room gun-first.

He had a fleeting glimpse of a swarthy Mexican wheeling from the doorway that led into the main room, and then he ducked and jerked the trigger as a knife sang past his head. The roar of the .45 shook the narrow room and the knife thrower hit the planks and lay twitching.

With a lunging stride Laramie was through the door, into the main room. He caught a glimpse of men standing momentarily frozen, glaring up from their work of tying

Bob Anders to a chair--Ely Harrison, another Mexican, and Mart Rawley.

For an infinitesimal tick of time the scene held--then blurred with gun-smoke as the .45s roared death across the narrow confines. Hot lead was a coal of hell burning its way through the flesh of Laramie's already wounded shoulder. Bob Anders lurched out of the chair, rolling clumsily toward the wall. The room was a mad welter of sound and smoke in the last light of gathering dusk.

Laramie half rolled behind the partial cover of a cast iron stove, drawing his second gun. The Mexican fled to the bunk-room, howling, his broken left arm flopping. Mart Rawley backed after him at a stumbling run, shooting as he went; crouched inside the door he glared, awaiting his chance. But Harrison, already badly wounded, had gone berserk. Disdaining cover, or touched with madness, he came storming across the room, shooting as he came, spattering blood at every step. His eyes flamed through the drifting fog of smoke like those of a rabid wolf.

Laramie raised himself to his full height and faced him. Searing lead whined past his ear, jerked at his shirt, stung his thigh; but his own gun was burning red and Harrison was swaying in his stride like a bull which feels the matador's steel. His last shot flamed almost in Laramie's face, and then at close range a bullet split the cold heart of the devil of San

Leon, and the greed and ambitions of Ely Harrison were over.

Laramie, with one loaded cartridge left in his last gun, leaned back against the wall, out of range of the bunk room.

"Come on out, Rawley," he called. "Harrison's dead. Yore game's played out."

The hidden gunman spat like an infuriated cat.

"No, my game ain't played out!" he yelled in a voice edged with blood-madness. "Not till I've wiped you out, you mangy stray. But before I kill you, I want you to know that you ain't the first Laramie I've sent to hell! I'd of thought you'd knowed me, in spite of these whiskers. I'm Rawlins, you fool! Killer Rawlins, that plugged yore horse-thief brother Luke in Santa Maria!"

"Rawlins!" snarled Laramie, suddenly white. "No wonder you knowed me!"

"Yes, Rawlins!" howled the gunman. "I'm the one that made friends with Luke Laramie and got him drunk till he told me all about this hide-out and the trails across the desert. Then I picked a fight with Luke when he was too drunk to stand, and killed him to keep his mouth shut! And what you goin' to do about it?"

"I'm going to kill you, you hell-buzzard!" gritted Laramie, lurching away from the wall as Rawlins came frothing through the door, with both guns blazing. Laramie

85

fired once from the hip. His last bullet ripped through Killer Rawlins' warped brain. Laramie looked down on him as he died, with his spurred heels drumming a death-march on the floor.

Frantic feet behind him brought him around to see a livid, swarthy face convulsed with fear and hate, a brown arm lifting a razor-edged knife. He had forgotten the Mexican. He threw up his empty pistol to guard the downward sweep of the sharp blade, then once more the blast of a six-gun shook the room. Jose Martinez of Chihuahua lifted one scream of invocation and blasphemy at some forgotten Aztec god, as his soul went speeding its way to hell.

Laramie turned and stared stupidly through the smoke-blurred dusk at a tall, slim figure holding a smoking gun. Others were pouring in through the kitchen. So brief had been the desperate fight that the men who had raced around the house at the first bellow of the guns, had just reached the scene. Laramie shook his head dazedly.

"Slim!" he muttered. "See if Bob's hurt!"

"Not me!" The sheriff answered for himself, struggling up to a sitting posture by the wall. "I fell outa the chair and rolled outa line when the lead started singin'. Cut me loose, somebody."

"Cut him loose, Slim," mumbled Laramie. "I'm kinda dizzy."

Stark silence followed the roar of the six-guns, silence that hurt Buck Laramie's ear-drums. Like a man in a daze he staggered to a chair and sank down heavily upon it. Scarcely knowing what he did he found himself muttering the words of a song he hated:

"When the folks heard that Brady was dead,

They all turned out, all dressed in red;

Marched down the street a-singin' a song:

'Brady's gone to hell with his Stetson on!'"

He was hardly aware when Bob Anders came and cut his blood-soaked shirt away and washed his wounds, dressing them as best he could with strips torn from his own shirt, and whisky from a jug found on the table. The bite of the alcohol roused Laramie from the daze that enveloped him, and a deep swig of the same medicine cleared his dizzy head.

Laramie rose stiffly; he glanced about at the dead men staring glassily in the lamplight, shuddered, and retched suddenly at the reek of the blood that blackened the planks.

"Let's get out in the open!"

As they emerged into the cool dusk, they were aware that the shooting had ceased. A voice was bawling loudly at the head of the canyon, though the distance made the words unintelligible.

Slim came running back through the dusk.

"They're makin' a parley, Bob!" he reported. "They want to know if they'll be give a fair trial if they surrender."

"I'll talk to 'em. Rest of you keep under cover."

The sheriff worked toward the head of the canyon until he was within earshot of the men in and about the tunnel, and shouted: "Are you hombres ready to give in?"

"What's yore terms?" bawled back the spokesman, recognizing the sheriff's voice.

"I ain't makin' terms. You'll all get a fair trial in an honest court. You better make up yore minds. I know they ain't a lot of you left. Harrison's dead and so is Rawley. I got forty men outside this canyon and enough inside, behind you, to wipe you out. Throw yore guns out here where I can see 'em, and come out with yore hands high. I'll give you till I count ten."

And as he began to count, rifles and pistols began clattering on the bare earth, and haggard, blood-stained, powder-blackened men rose from behind rocks with their hands in the air, and came out of the tunnel in the same manner.

"We quits," announced the spokesman. "Four of the boys are laying back amongst the rocks too shot up to move under their own power. One's got a broke laig where his horse fell on him. Some of the rest of us need to have wounds dressed."

Laramie and Slim and the punchers came out of cover, with guns trained on the weary outlaws, and at a shout from Anders, the men outside came streaming through the tunnel, whooping vengefully.

"No mob-stuff," warned Anders, as the men grabbed the prisoners and bound their hands, none too gently. "Get those four wounded men out of the rocks, and we'll see what we can do for them."

Presently, a curious parade came filing through the tunnel into the outer valley where twilight still lingered. And as Laramie emerged from that dark tunnel, he felt as if his dark and sinister past had fallen from him like a worn-out coat.

One of the four wounded men who had been brought through the tunnel on crude stretchers rigged out of rifles and coats was in a talkative mood. Fear and the pain of his wound had broken his nerve entirely and he was overflowing with information.

"I'll tell you anything you want to know! Put in a good word for me at my trial, and I'll spill the works!" he declaimed, ignoring the sullen glares of his hardier companions.

"How did Harrison get mixed up in this deal?" demanded the sheriff.

"Mixed, hell! He planned the whole thing. He was cashier in the bank when the Laramies robbed it; the real ones, I mean. If it hadn't been for that robbery, old Brown would soon found out that Harrison was stealin' from him. But the Laramies killed Brown and give Harrison a chance to cover his tracks. They got blamed for the dough he'd stole, as well as the money they'd actually taken.

"That give Harrison an idee how to be king of San Leon. The Laramies had acted as scapegoats for him once, and he aimed to use 'em again. But he had to wait till he could get to be president of the bank, and had taken time to round up a gang."

"So he'd ruin the ranchers, give mortgages and finally get their outfits, and then send his coyotes outa the country and be king of San Leon," broke in Laramie. "We know that part of it. Where'd Rawlins come in?"

"Harrison knowed him years ago, on the Rio Grande. When Harrison aimed to raise his gang, he went to Mexico and found Rawlins. Harrison knowed the real Laramies had a secret hide-out, so Rawlins made friends with Luke Laramie, and--"

"We know all about that," interrupted Anders with a quick glance at Buck.

"Yeah? Well, everything was bueno till word come from Mexico that Buck Laramie was ridin' up from there. Harrison got skittish. He thought Laramie was comin' to take toll for his brother. So he sent Rawlins to waylay Laramie. Rawlins missed, but later went on to San Leon to try again. He shot you instead, Anders. Word was out to get you, anyway. You'd been prowlin' too close to our hide-out to suit Harrison.

"Harrison seemed to kinda go locoed when first he heard Laramie was headin' this way. He made us pull that fool stunt of a fake bank hold-up to pull wool over folks's eyes more'n ever. Hell, nobody suspected him anyway. Then he risked comin' out here. But he was panicky and wanted us to git ready to make a clean sweep tonight and pull out. When Laramie got away from us this mornin', Harrison decided he'd ride to Mexico with us.

"Well, when the fightin' had started, Harrison and Rawley stayed out a sight. Nothin' they could do, and they hoped we'd be able to break out of the canyon. They didn't want to be seen and recognized. If it should turn out Laramie hadn't told anybody he was head of the gang, Harrison would be able to stay on, then."

Preparations were being made to start back to San Leon with the prisoners, when a sheepish looking delegation headed by Mayor Jim Watkins approached Laramie. Watkins hummed and hawed with embarrassment, and finally blurted out, with typical Western bluntness:

"Look here, Laramie, we owe you somethin' now, and we're just as hot too pay our debts as you are to pay yours. Harrison had a small ranch out a ways from town, which he ain't needin' no more, and he ain't got no heirs, so we can get it easy enough. We thought if you was aimin', maybe, to

91

stay around San Leon, we'd like powerful well to make you a present of that ranch, and kinda help you get a start in the cow business. And we don't want the fifty thousand Waters said you aimed to give us. You've wiped out that debt."

A curious moroseness had settled over Laramie, a futile feeling of anti-climax, and a bitter yearning he did not understand. He felt old and weary, a desire to be alone, and an urge to ride away over the rim of the world and forget--he did not even realize what it was he wanted to forget.

"Thanks." he muttered. "I'm paying that fifty thousand back to the men it belonged to. And I'll be movin' on tomorrow."

"Where to?"

He made a helpless, uncertain gesture.

"You think it over," urged Watkins, turning away. Men were already mounting, moving down the trail. Anders touched Laramie's sleeve.

"Let's go. Buck. You need some attention on them wounds."

"Go ahead. Bob. I'll be along. I wanta kind set here and rest."

Anders glanced sharply at him and then made a hidden gesture to Slim Jones, and turned away. The cavalcade moved down the trail in the growing darkness, armed men riding toward a new era of peace and prosperity; gaunt, haggard bound men riding toward the penitentiary and the gallows.

Laramie sat motionless, his empty hands hanging limp on his knees. A vital chapter in his life had closed, leaving him without a goal. He had kept his vow. Now he had no plan or purpose to take its place.

Slim Jones, standing nearby, not understanding Laramie's mood, but not intruding on it, started to speak. Then both men lifted their heads at the unexpected rumble of wheels.

"A buckboard!" ejaculated Slim.

"No buckboard ever come up that trail," snorted Laramie.

"One's comin' now; and who d'you think? Old Joel, by golly. And look who's drivin'!"

Laramie's heart gave a convulsive leap and then started pounding as he saw the slim supple figure beside the old rancher. She pulled up near them and handed the lines to Slim, who sprang to help her down.

"Biggest fight ever fit in San Leon County!" roared Waters, "and I didn't git to fire a shot. Cuss a busted laig, anyway!"

"You done a man's part, anyway, Joel," assured Laramie; and then he forgot Joel Waters entirely, in the miracle of seeing Judy Anders standing before him, smiling gently, her hand outstretched and the rising moon melting her soft hair to golden witch-fire.

"I'm sorry for the way I spoke to you today," she said softly. "I've been bitter about things that were none of your fault."

"D-don't apologize, please," he stuttered, inwardly cursing himself because of his confusion. The touch of her slim, firm hand sent shivers through his frame and he knew all at once what that empty, gnawing yearning was; the more poignant now, because so unattainable.

"You saved my neck. Nobody that does that needs to apologize. You was probably right, anyhow. Er--uh--Bob went down the trail with the others. You must have missed him."

"I saw him and talked to him," she said softly. "He said you were behind them. I came on, expecting to meet you."

He was momentarily startled. "You came on to meet me? Oh, of course. Joel would want to see how bad shot up I was." He achieved a ghastly excuse for a laugh.

"Mr. Waters wanted to see you, of course. But I--Buck, I wanted to see you, too."

She was leaning close to him, looking up at him, and he was dizzy with the fragrance and beauty of her; and in his dizziness said the most inane and idiotic thing he could possibly have said.

"To see me?" he gurgled wildly. "What--what you want to see me for?"

She seemed to draw away from him and her voice was a bit too precise.

"I wanted to apologize for my rudeness this morning," she said, a little distantly.

"I said don't apologize to me," he gasped. "You saved my life--and I--I--Judy, dang it, I love you!"

It was out--the amazing statement, blurted out involuntarily. He was frozen by his own audacity, stunned and paralyzed. But she did not seem to mind. Somehow he found she was in his arms, and numbly he heard her saying: "I love you too, Buck. I've loved you ever since I was a little girl, and we went to school together. Only I've tried to force myself not to think of you for the past six years. But I've loved the memory of you--that's why it hurt me so to think that you'd gone bad--as I thought you had. That horse I brought you--it wasn't altogether because you'd helped Bob that I brought it to you. It--it was partly because of my own feeling. Oh, Buck, to learn you're straight and honorable is like having a black shadow lifted from between us. You'll never leave me, Buck?"

"Leave you?" Laramie gasped. "Just long enough to find Watkins and tell him I'm takin' him up on a proposition he made me, and then I'm aimin' on spendin' the rest of my life makin' you happy." The rest was lost in a perfectly natural sound.

"Kissin'!" beamed Joel Waters, sitting in his buckboard and gently manipulating his wounded leg. "Reckon they'll be a marryin' in these parts purty soon, Slim."

"Don't tell me yo're figgerin' on gittin' hitched?" inquired Slim, pretending to misunderstand, but grinning behind his hand.

"You go light on that sarcastic tone. I'm liable to git married any day now. It's just a matter of time till I decide what type of woman would make me the best wife."

THE END

www.ingramcontent.com/pod-product-compliance
Lightning Source LLC
Chambersburg PA
CBHW030134260626
47156CB00008B/2942